MEET THE AUTHOR – TERRY DEARY

What is your favourite animal?
A rat
What is your favourite boy's name?
Marmaduke
What is your favourite girl's name?
Bertha
What is your favourite food?
Horse
What is your favourite music?
Bagpipes
What is your favourite hobby?
Singing to bagpipes

MEET THE ILLUSTRATOR – STEVE DONALD

What is your favourite animal?
A goldfish
What is your favourite boy's name?
Kieran
What is your favourite girl's name?
Elizabeth
What is your favourite food?
Scrambled eggs
What is your favourite music?
'70s pop music
What is your favourite hobby?
Playing on my computer

To Connie,
for putting up with my jokes

SD

Contents

Streatley, Berkshire, England 1

1 Mrs Rundle's Brainwave 3

2 A Bargain Buy 11

3 Mrs Barclay's Story 17

4 The Wardrobe Changes Hands 23

5 Unwanted Visitors 35

6 Ghostly Goings-On 41

7 Things that Go Bump ... 47

8 Peace at Last? 55

Afterword 59

What do you think? 62

Streatley, Berkshire, England

1937

Ghosts should be scary. They shock and terrify anyone who sees them. So why do so many people try to see a ghost? They love to visit a castle or stay in a hotel that has a ghost. They would even buy a wardrobe with a ghost in it …

Chapter 1
Mrs Rundle's Brainwave

Mr Rundle was eating his breakfast at *The Dog and Duck*. He drank a cup of tea, bit into his toast and looked at the adverts on the back page of the newspaper. Mrs Rundle sat on the other side of the table and read the headlines on the front page.

"I see the Chinese are sending 300,000 troops to fight the Japanese," she said.

"Very nice, dear," Mr Rundle replied.

"I do wish you'd listen when I'm talking to you," Mrs Rundle snapped.

"Yes, I read all about that in the paper," Mr Rundle replied.

Mrs Rundle leant forward. "There is a great big spider crawling up your nose to eat your brain!" she said.

"Really, dear?"

"But it's run off again because it can't find any brains in there," she went on.

"Ah, that'll be all right, dear." He nodded and turned the page.

"I've put poison in your tea," Mrs Rundle said next.

"Good grief!" Mr Rundle yelled.

Mrs Rundle jumped. "I was only joking. I only said it to make you sit up and listen!"

"Would you believe it?" he shouted.

"Believe what?" Mrs Rundle said.

"It's Mrs Barclay!" he cried.

"What's she done now?"

"She's put an advert in the paper!"

"How exciting," Mrs Rundle said with a sigh.

"No, listen! It says ...

"'FOR SALE – Wardrobe, with it's own ghost. I will be happy to deliver this to anyone who wants to buy it. The ghost will be more at home if it is made to feel welcome. Please write to Mrs Barclay', and it gives the address."

"I always thought she was a funny woman," Mrs Rundle said.

"But you said she was a wonderful woman and very charming, even though she was so very rich. Don't you remember?" Mr Rundle put down the newspaper and stuck his pipe in his mouth.

"Buy that wardrobe, Mr Rundle," his wife ordered.

Her husband opened his mouth and his pipe almost fell into his teacup. "Why should I?"

"We want to make *The Dog and Duck* a bit smarter, don't we? It'll add interest to the place. People will come from miles around to stay in a room that has a wardrobe with a ghost in it," she told him. And she folded her fat arms.

"Where do we put it while we've got workmen in *The Dog and Duck*?" asked her husband.

"In the shed at the bottom of the garden. I'll phone Mrs Barclay now before someone else snaps it up," Mrs Rundle said. "*You* can do the washing up."

Chapter 2
A Bargain Buy

Mrs Barclay was a small, neat woman. She wore a flowery dress and her grey hair was set in waves. She opened the door with care. Her face lit up when she saw the Rundles.

"Oh, my dears, do come in!" she cried in a high voice.

"You have to open the door yourself, Mrs Barclay?" Mrs Rundle asked. "Where are all the servants?"

"We haven't got any!" Mrs Barclay said with a sigh. "They've all left because of the ghost. Even Martha, the cook, says she can't stand any more and she's off too. But come in and have a look at the wardrobe."

"It's a beautiful wardrobe," she went on as she led the way up the stairs. "I got it in a sale 3 years ago. It was just a normal wardrobe. But I liked it and bought it. Only cost me 10 pounds."

"Oh, Mr Rundle will give you 20 pounds," Mrs Rundle told her. "Won't you, Mr Rundle?"

"Why not make it 30 pounds?" her husband said rather crossly.

Mrs Barclay stopped at the top of the stairs. "I've had so many offers. First came the phone calls and today the letters began

to arrive. I'll show them to you if you like. But have a look at the wardrobe first."

She led the way into the bedroom. Everything was very grand, the rich carpet, the pretty paper on the walls and the satin on the bed. But there was dust everywhere.

"You've lost your maids too, I see," Mrs Rundle said.

"Everyone has left and all because of the wardrobe!"

Chapter 3
Mrs Barclay's Story

They all looked at the tall wardrobe. It had drawers and mirrors and looked the same as any other wardrobe.

"It'll look nice in the best bedroom at *The Dog and Duck*," Mrs Rundle smiled.

"Everyone will want to see it," Mrs Barclay said with a laugh. "So many people want to buy it. You'll have lots more visitors."

"We never thought of that," said Mrs Rundle. This wasn't true.

"I'll show you some of my letters," Mrs Barclay went on. She led the way into the living room, sank into an armchair and rang a bell. A woman with a white apron came out from the kitchen. She looked

grumpy. "Tea for 3, please Martha," Mrs
Barclay said.

Martha, the cook, went back to make it.
Mrs Barclay said, "We had no trouble for 2
years. Then friends who stayed in that
room began to ask about the wardrobe.
*Was there something odd about it? Why did
the doors keep opening and shutting?
Would we mind if they went home?* Why,
my dear, at this rate I'll have no friends
left."

"Did you see anything yourself?" Mr
Rundle asked.

"Oh, yes. My butler, Mr East, and I spent
an evening there. We checked it on the
outside for secret panels and springs.
Nothing! But when Mr East said he would
look inside, something terrible happened.
The door flew across the room and smashed

into that table mirror! We were scared stiff.
I nearly fainted."

"I'd have died," Mrs Rundle nodded.

"But we had woken up the ghost," Mrs
Barclay went on.

"Risen from the grave," Mrs Rundle
added.

"Risen from the grave! That's just what
Mr East said. Then, one night, a ghostly
shape came out of the wardrobe ..."

Chapter 4

The Wardrobe Changes Hands

"How big was it?" Mr Rundle asked.

"Almost 8 foot high" said Mrs Barclay.

"What! An 8 foot ghostly shape!"

"No, no, the wardrobe is 8 foot high," said Mrs Barclay. "And the ghostly shape was about 5 foot. It was a little old man with a funny hat."

"What did this ghostly shape do?" Mr Rundle asked.

"He walked downstairs and went out of the front door," Mrs Barclay told them.

"Ghosts walk *through* doors," Mr Rundle said. Everyone knew that.

"Well this one didn't. He opened the door and slammed it behind him! Quite rude he was. Then the wardrobe doors kept opening and banging shut again. No-one could get to sleep. The servants started to leave! The ghostly shape hated the butler and kicked him on the shins. He left too, of course."

"Can't blame him," Mr Rundle said.

"So the wardrobe has to go. Still, I never thought so many people would want it."

She pointed to a table. Letters were sorted into neat piles. Mrs Barclay walked

across to them and began to read parts of
them.

"Look at this one …

can I have my
money back
if the ghost
doesn't appear?

"And this …

*I am a professor
of ghostly studies …*

"And this ...

> We are four ladies
> living alone and we
> think the ghost might
> protect our house ...

"And this ...

Do you think your ghost would be happy in a small, modern house?

"Well, the *ghost* might be happy in a modern house but I don't think the wardrobe would fit. And look at this!" Mrs Barclay passed another letter to her friend.

Mrs Rundle read it. She looked amazed. How very rude! She read it to her husband.

Dear Mrs Barclay,

I am very interested in your wardrobe and you. Will you marry me?

"Well I never! What a nerve!" said Mr Rundle.

"I've had lots of advice," Mrs Barclay went on.

Don't lock the wardrobe ...

Place a nice
comfortable chair
beside the wardrobe
for the ghost.

*There is almost
certainly treasure
inside ...*

"And look at this ...

If I were you I'd
keep it. You'll
never have
another wardrobe
like that!

"I ask you!"

Mrs Rundle put the letters back on the table. "*We'll* buy the wardrobe, won't we, Harry dear?"

"Er ... well ..."

"Harry will give you *50* pounds, won't you, Harry dear?"

"I'll deliver it to you tomorrow," Mrs Barclay said. "There are some people from the newspapers who want to spend the night in that room."

Chapter 5
Unwanted Visitors

The van pulled up at *The Dog and Duck* with 3 men in it. Mrs Barclay pulled up behind in her Morris car.

Mrs Rundle looked on as the men carried the wardrobe to the shed at the bottom of the garden. "How did the newspaper men get on?" she asked.

"Most odd," Mrs Barclay said. "We had reporters from two local newspapers and one of the London papers too."

"Oooh! You'll be famous!" Mrs Rundle told her.

"Well they didn't want to take my photo," Mrs Barclay sniffed. "They only wanted photos of the wardrobe!"

"And did the little man come out? The one in the funny hat?"

"Nothing happened for an hour," Mrs Barclay said in a low voice. "Then all at once there were sounds from inside the wardrobe. A reporter shone a torch on the floor and there was a button that had not been there before. Then I saw him. 'He's there!' I cried. The little man came out of the wardrobe and ran across the room."

"Did the reporters see him?" Mrs Rundle asked.

"No," Mrs Barclay said sadly. "They were too slow." She looked down the garden path of *The Dog and Duck* and saw the men close the shed door.

"Well, I see it's found a safe home. I had so many offers ..."

"Oh! I mustn't forget to pay you," Mrs Rundle said and pulled 50 1-pound notes from her pocket.

"It would be cheap at *twice* the price," Mrs Barclay said, tucking the money away deep inside her handbag. "You'll see. You won't be able to move for visitors to your inn."

But, when the visitors came, they were not the sort the Rundles wanted.

Chapter 6
Ghostly Goings-On

The wardrobe at the bottom of the garden didn't bother the Rundles ... but the visitors did. Mr Rundle was filling a glass with beer behind the bar when a young man with a large cap ran into the bar.

"The ghost!" he wailed. "There's a ghost out there! It's horrible. It's disgusting!"

The bar was full. Everyone rushed to the door. The young man had to move out of the way, fast.

Another young man was yelling, "The back garden. The shed! It came out of the shed wailing and screaming!"

The crowd from the bar pushed and shoved to be the first to see the ghost. People in the same street came to their doors to find out what was going on. Soon there were 50 people standing on the back lawn of the inn.

No-one said a word. In the silence a white shape came out of the shed. It was tall and it flapped in the light wind. Some people backed away. Someone screamed.

The ghost began to make a sound that was ... ghostly.

"Hoooo! Hoooo!"

It had two large patches on the front of its head where eyes should have been. It turned towards the crowd on the lawn and began to move towards them. Even the brave ones began to panic as the cries of the crowd and the wails of the ghost grew louder.

Then the ghost tripped and fell forward. There was a ripping sound as the white sheet tore and the young man inside fell flat on his face. He was hooting with laughter!

"Caw!" he cried. "You should have seen your faces!"

The angry crowd moved forward. He dashed down the garden, past the shed and over the wall that led to the railway line. He was still laughing as he ran off into the night.

Chapter 7
Things that Go Bump ...

"It's no good, Harry," one of the drinkers told Mr Rundle as they all went back inside. "You'll be the victim of every joker in the county as long as you have that thing in your shed."

Mr Rundle gave a sigh. "You're right. There's a room I can put it in upstairs. I'll bring it in first thing tomorrow."

But the Rundles had a restless night. Stones rained down on the roof of their shed. Voices hooted through their letter-box. Screaming and howling went on all night. The police had to be called in to get rid of the jokers.

Next morning Mr Rundle, with the help of some friends, dragged the wardrobe into

the inn and up the stairs to the best
bedroom.

The owners of *The Dog and Duck* looked
forward to a restful night.

But that night Mr Rundle woke with a start. He was sure that he had heard a rumbling sound from the best bedroom. He slid his feet into an old pair of slippers and crept towards the door. The floor creaked under his feet but his wife did not wake up. She was fast asleep and snoring.

He opened the bedroom door and it groaned. There was a little light from the moon. Mr Rundle wished he had a poker with him.

His mouth was dry. He put his ear against the door of the best bedroom. He heard the creaking noises that the old inn often made in the night, but nothing else.

When he pushed the door open something soft brushed against his face. He almost screamed with fear. But it was just a dressing gown hanging behind the door.

The wardrobe was silent, but Mr Rundle felt it was the silence of an animal waiting to spring.

He backed out of the room and padded back to bed. Was that the sound of laughter coming from the best bedroom?

Chapter 8
Peace at Last?

Mr Rundle tried to laugh about it next morning when he told his wife about the noises.

"I expect the ghost's looking for something," Mrs Rundle told her husband.

"Yes, dear," he replied.

"Take the wardrobe apart and you may find the treasure," she said.

"Yes, dear."

"Well? What are you waiting for?"

"You want me to do it *now*?"

The woman folded her arms. Mr Rundle knew who was boss. It took him an hour to take the wardrobe apart. It took him two hours to put it back together.

"No treasure," he told his wife.

And after that there was no ghost either. The little old man in the funny hat had been driven away.

"50 pounds is a lot to pay for a plain old wardrobe," Mrs Rundle said a week later. The fuss had died down and the visitors had stopped coming to see it. "Why did you have to take it apart?" she asked.

"Sorry, dear," Mr Rundle said in a low voice.

Mr Rundle read his paper. "There's a nice wardrobe for sale here ..." he began.

Mrs Rundle folded her arms.

"Just a thought," her husband said with a sigh.

Afterword

Some six months later Mr Rundle shut up the bar for the night. He wiped the last table clean and went into the kitchen to make his cocoa. Then he went upstairs. Mrs Rundle was staying with her sister that week. He had to work harder in the bar, but at least he had a bit of peace in the evening.

Why not sleep in the best bedroom? Mr Rundle slipped under the cool sheets and sipped the cocoa. He read the newspaper then folded it and dropped it by the side of the bed. Then he wiped away the cocoa from round his mouth and turned off the light. He gave a sigh – he was a happy man. Only a faint light from a street lamp lit the room.

An owl hooted in the woods and a cat yowled in the garden.

A door creaked in the bedroom ...

Mr Rundle's eyes flew open. In the half-dark he saw the door of the wardrobe swing open. He saw a tweed jacket. It could have been his own jacket hanging there – or it could have belonged to the little old man with the funny hat.

Mr Rundle didn't stay to find out. He spent the night in the kitchen with the fire blazing and all the lights turned on.

When the sun rose and the first bus arrived in the village, his wife found him sitting at the table. There was a sheet of paper in his shaking hand. He'd written just 3 words:

Ghost for sale ...

What do you think?

Was there a ghost?

The wardrobe had been mended at some time – a new panel had been fitted into its floor. But perhaps the old one was rotten.

Had the ghost hidden something in the wardrobe when he was alive and put the new panel over it?

Had someone else found this hidden "something" and taken it away?

Was it money or was it treasure?

Is that why the grumpy little man with the funny hat came back night after night?

We can only guess.

Can you explain it?

Was Mrs Barclay telling fibs about her wardrobe? Remember, the newspaper men never saw her ghost. No-one talked to her servants and asked them what they thought.

But, why would Mrs Barclay want to lie about the ghost?

Here is one possible answer which fits the facts. But it has nothing to do with ghosts.

Perhaps Mrs Barclay needed money. (A lot of rich people lost money in the 1930s.) One by one the servants left because she couldn't pay their wages.

She thought up a plan to make money. (It would not only bring her some cash – it would also explain to everyone why such a "rich" woman had no servants.)

Mrs Barclay buys 10 old wardrobes for (say) 5 pounds each. She puts an advert for a wardrobe "with its own ghost" in the newspaper. She has lots of offers. Many people are willing to pay 50 pounds (or more) for what is just a piece of junk – if they get a ghost with it. She sells the 10 wardrobes to the 10 best offers. "This is the one and only wardrobe with its own ghost," she tells each one.

Result? She makes nearly 500 pounds.

Possible? What do *you* think?

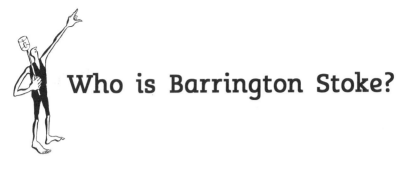

Who is Barrington Stoke?

Barrington Stoke went from place to place with his lamp in his hand. Everywhere he went, he told stories to children. Some were happy, some were sad, some were funny and some were scary.

The children always wanted more. When it got dark, they had to go home to bed. They went to look for Barrington Stoke the next day, but he had gone.

The children never forgot the stories. They told them to each other and to their children and their grandchildren. You see, good stories are magic and they can live for ever.

If you loved this story, why don't you read ...

The Hat Trick

by Terry Deary

Is there something you'll remember for as long as you'll live? When Seaburn football team meet their rivals, Jud has to step in as goalie. Can Jud save the day?

4u2read.ok!

If you loved this story, why don't you read ...

Grow Up, Dad!
by Narinder Dhami

Do you ever feel as if your dad doesn't understand you? Robbie does. His dad just doesn't know how he feels. Until one day, with a bit of magic, things change forever ...

4u2read.ok!

You can order this book directly from our website
www.barringtonstoke.co.uk

If you loved this story, why don't you read ...

Pitt Street Pirates

by Terry Deary

Have you ever dreamed of finding a long-lost treasure? Meet the Pitt Street Pirates – a group of friends with just one thing in mind – to sail the lakes in their local park in search of gold. But how will they put their plans into action?

4u2read.ok!

You can order this book directly from our website
www.barringtonstoke.co.uk

If you loved this story, why don't you read ...

The Best in the World

by Chris Powling

Have you ever wanted to push yourself to the limit? Lucas and Jeb are ready to do the "Triple" and become the best trapeze artists in the world. But will they risk their lives to follow a dream?

4u2read.ok!